This book belongs to

_ _ _ _ _ _ _ _ _ _ _ _

Design - Douglas Strachan
Printing - Oriental Press, Dubai

Published by

Publishing

GW Publishing
PO Box 6091, Thatcham, Berks, RG19 8XZ Tel +44 (0) 1635 268080
www.gwpublishing.com

ISBN 978-0-9554145-4-1

The Jammy Spider

Written by David Gall
Illustrated by Douglas Strachan

In a cupboard in a kitchen in a house ... upon a street, lives a little hairy spider you know ... the type you dread to meet!

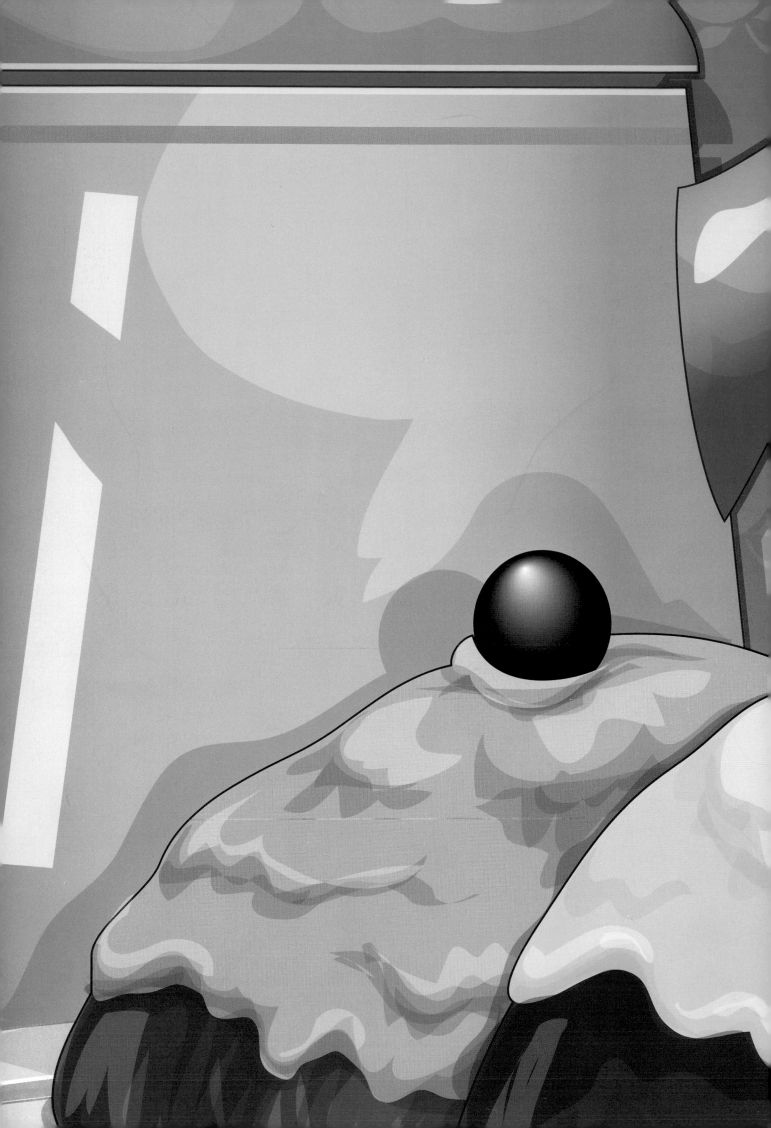

Sam, the cheeky spider
likes to have some fun,
by dropping from the ceiling
and landing on a bun.

"I wonder what makes them jump?"
Sam would ponder to himself,
as a voice let out a little scream
while he dangled from a shelf.

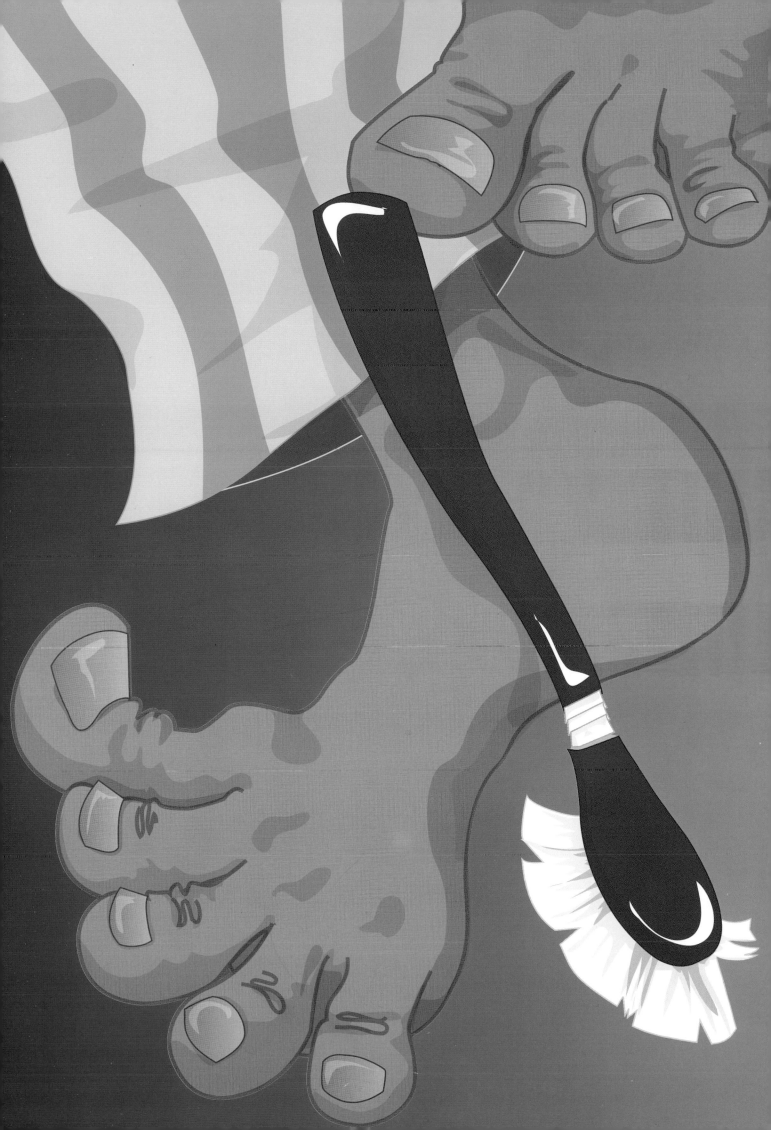

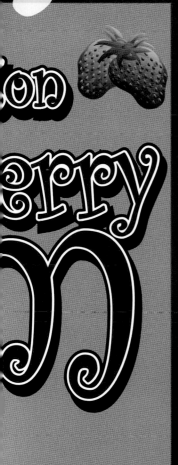

Sam was feeling hungry
as he crossed the kitchen floor,
then climbing up he saw some jam
through an open cupboard door.

He quickly raced up to the jar
which seemed so big and wide,
round and round its base he ran
trying to get inside.

So up the glass he clambered,
but... before he reached its top....

...the jar was snatched down from the shelf then the lid went...
POP!

All Sam could do was hold on tight
as jam oozed down the side,
his legs got stuck as he tried to move
there was nowhere he could hide.

Sam pulled and tugged really hard
but wasn't getting very far,
when suddenly a knife appeared
and scooped him from the jar.

His legs coiled up just like a ball
as he fell over on his head,
poor Sam was in an awful mess
stuck on a slice of bread.

As the knife went back and forwards
Sam was spread out flat,
he looked just like a strawberry
then another slice went ...

Sam was in total darkness
squashed in between the bread ...

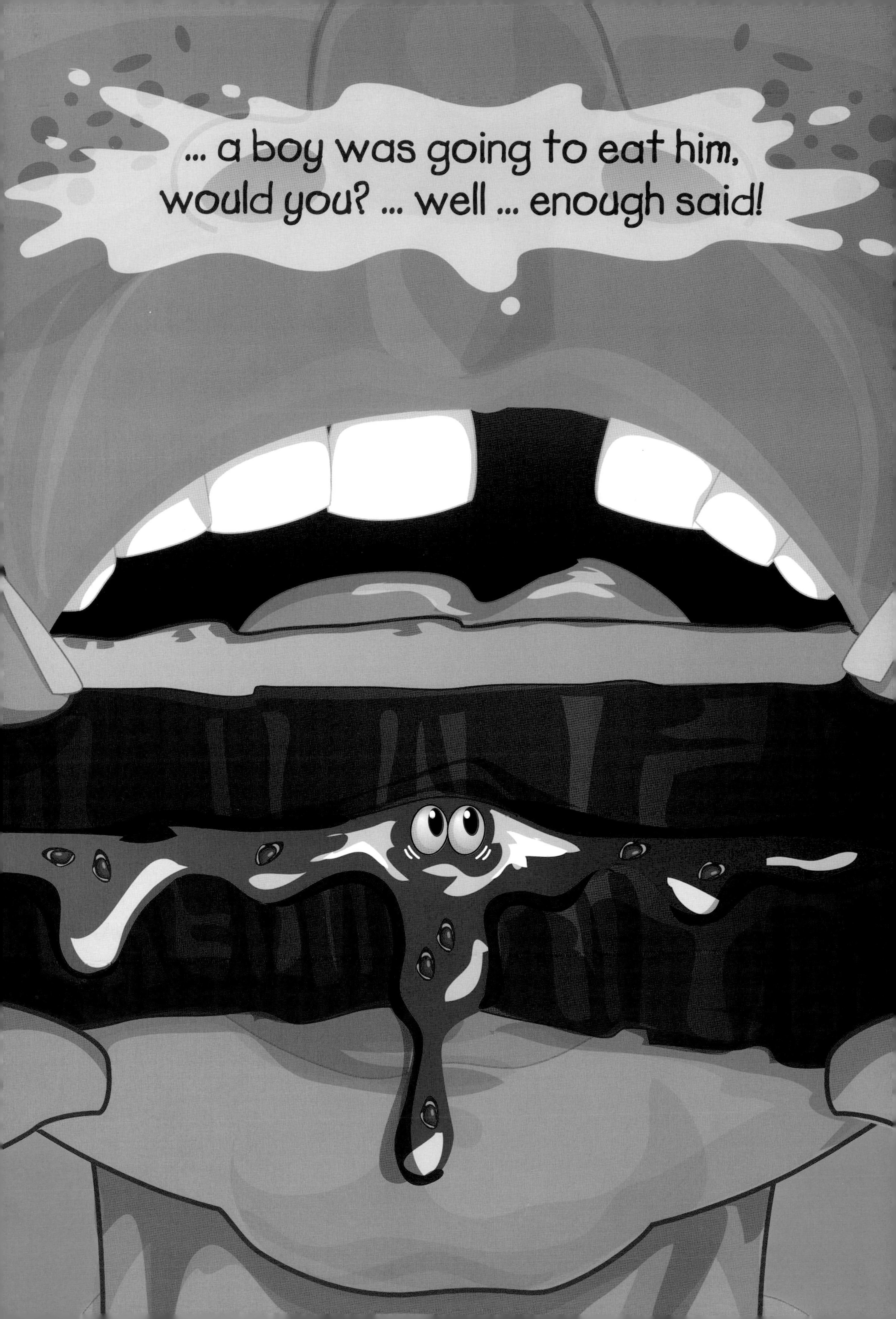
... a boy was going to eat him, would you? ... well ... enough said!

"Oh not another sandwich!"
A voice let out a roar,
Sam peeped out between the slices
as they tumbled to the floor.

"Now look what you have done!"
the voice boomed out,
to Sam it was such a din ...

... peering out ... it went dark again
as he landed in the bin.

Now Sam was really lucky
the sandwich split in two,
as he lay amongst the garbage
Sam thought ...
"I know what to do!".

He stayed in the bin all night long
and licked himself quite clean,
then just before the sun came up
he crawled away unseen.

Sam was feeling happy
as he crept across the floor,
when he saw that jar of jam again
through the open cupboard door.

He was a very clever spider
so across the shelf he raced,
he liked that strawberry jam so much
he had to have another taste

He ran around, then up the jar
but ... before he reached its top,
he hung on tight and waited
until the lid went ...

POP!

So in a cupboard in every kitchen ...
in every house ... on every street,
lives a little hairy spider
you know ...
the type you would dread to eat!

Hoots Mon

SAM'S SPIDER SPORTS

What Sam get's up to when nobody is looking!

DIVING

TRAMPOLINING

SKIING

SKATING